DON'T TOUCH TULLY!

Available in the Tales of Tully series

Tully's Life
This heart-warming story follows the journey of Tully from street dog to much-loved family pet, teaching young readers about the importance of kindness, understanding and hope.

Tully Takes Off!
Tully has arrived in her new home with her new grown-up, but she does not like it one bit! When Tully sees an opportunity to go back to her old life on the streets - the only life she has known up to now - she takes it with both paws. With a search underway, it is up to her new grown-up to work out what Tully needs and help get her safely home.

Tully and the Sad Day
Tully has woken up feeling grey and cloudy inside and she does not know what to do. She cannot help her big feeling because she does not know what it is. As her different feelings begin to work together in the wrong way, it is up to Tully's grown-up to help her to understand what she needs.

Go To Sleep Tully!
It is night time and Tully is tired, but she does not want to go to sleep. Her new grown-up knows that Tully is trying every trick she can to avoid going go to bed! With lots of adventures planned and Tully needing her rest, Tully's grown-up needs to find a way to help Tully learn to not be so worried about bedtime.

Tully and the Midnight Feast
Tully is a newly-adopted dog settling in with her new grown-up. Since her arrival, her snacks have started mysteriously disappearing from the cupboard and appearing under her bed, she seems to have forgotten her manners, and there are days when she just cannot stop eating! Tully and her grown-up need to work together to help Tully with her worries about food.

Tully and the Scary Day
Tully has woken up feeling scared. She isn't really sure why, but today feels like a very scary day, and she just wants to hide. Tully's grown-up is thankfully there to help Tully manage her big feelings and see that the day is not so scary after all.

Don't Touch Tully!
Tully is settling in with her new grown-up. She has learned that the new grown-up is a safe person and she enjoys strokes and cuddles with them. Then Tully starts to meet new people, who want to show her how loved she is. Unfortunately, Tully doesn't feel the same about people she does not know and trust. It is up to Tully's grown-up to find a way to help Tully with her big feelings and to be Tully's voice, when she can't use hers.

Tully and the Tummy Ache
Tully has a tummy ache and it's making her feel quite grumpy. She doesn't want to eat or drink, and she can't get comfortable. Her tummy is sore and it's getting worse! Tully is in a toilet muddle. So, Tully and her grown-up work together to sort the muddle out and help Tully to cure her tummy ache.

Tully's Birthday
It's Tully's birthday, and her grown-up has planned a special day for her, but Tully doesn't feel like celebrating. As the day begins to unfold, so do Tully's big feelings. Tully doesn't know what to do about the big feelings, so she does a bad thing. Luckily, Tully's grown-up is there to help her feel better about herself, and enjoy the rest of her birthday.

Listen, Tully!
Tully does not always like to listen, especially when her grown-up is trying to stop her having fun. Tully decides that instead of listening, she can be in charge. But when things start to go wrong, Tully and her grown-up need to work out how Tully can begin to find listening a little bit easier.

Tully and the Makeover
Tully has been having lots of fun playing in the mud, but now her grown-up says she has to have a bath. Oh dear! Tully is not sure she wants one of those. She is feeling a bit nervous about what is going to happen to her, but Tully's grown-up shows her that there is nothing to worry about. Having a bath is a good thing after all.

Tully and Vera
Tully has moved in with her new grown-up but she is missing her foster carer, Vera. Tully is struggling to understand why she had to leave, and whether it is okay to have big feelings about Vera. It is up to Tully's grown-up to try and help her to understand loss and endings and why, sometimes, they have to happen to make space for new beginnings.

Tully and the Chase
Tully loves to be chased. It gives her a feeling of excitement which starts off as being fun, but one day the excited feeling suddenly and very quickly becomes a feeling which is too big. Instead of feeling excited, Tully starts to feel scared. Tully and her grown-up need to work out how they can play Tully's exciting game without it becoming a bit too much for her, and causing a muddle.

Tully at Christmas
Things are starting to feel a bit different in Tully's house and all around outside. Tully's grown-up looks different, strange lights are appearing everywhere and people have started putting their gardens indoors! Tully is not sure what to make of this thing called Christmas – she just wants everything to stay the same. What can Tully's grown-up do to make Christmas-time a nicer time for both of them?

Tully Goes on Holiday
Tully has gone on a holiday with her grown-up. After a difficult start, things seem to be going well. But when the fairground opens up, with all its flashing lights, loud music and food smells, Tully's big feelings get the better of her, making her want to run. And she does! Tully's grown-up needs to find her in time to show her that holidays can be fun after all.

Tully and the New Rules
Tully likes lots of things about living in a house with her grown-up, but one thing she really doesn't like is all the rules! Tully thinks the rules are all very boring and her grown-up must want to stop her from having fun. One day Tully breaks her least favourite rule, and something bad happens. Tully doesn't know what to do! Can Tully's grown-up get to the bottom of this muddle so it doesn't happen again?

Don't Touch Tully!

TALES OF TULLY

Jess van der Hoech

Trauma Tools
& Training

ISBN-13 978-1-06-86917-1-3
Editing by Sarah Ogden
www.jvtraumatools.co.uk

Acknowledgements

As always, to my trusted editor Sarah Ogden for all that you do to make these books come to life. I will never fully know what goes on behind the scenes, but it is a joy to work alongside you on these projects. Thank you.

Thank you to my supervisor Linda Hoggan for your continued support, encouragement, discussion and much-welcomed feedback on this series. I learn so much from you and the knowledge I have gained form our conversations has been invaluable across my practice, the books and now this series. Thank you.

Thank you to Laura Benham, for your support in giving me feedback, the searching questions, your friendship and of course, the countless conversations about dogs, the content of which has become quite useful! Thank you.

To the children and families who I meet in my therapy room, from whom I have learned more about hope and healing than any course could ever teach me. Your input, ideas, questions and answers are so valuable to me and I will be forever grateful. Thank you.

Preface

The *Tales of Tully* series is based on the adoption of an ex street dog from Bosnia who came to live with me in September 2023. Watching her try to settle and adapt from everything she had previously known to fit in with a new way of life began to present a number of ideas as to how to communicate such difficulties that can be experienced, to others who are in the process of adopting or who have adopted children. The aim of the series is to provide an opportunity to explore different situations, circumstances, feelings and experiences, finding new ways of communicating and understanding each other, through the voice of Tully.

For children who have experienced early trauma, physical touch can be a huge issue. To some children, neither adults or touch have been safe experiences, meaning that both can be unwanted. Sensory issues can mean that even gentle touch is physically painful to the child and in anticipation of touch happening, fight, flight and freeze behaviours can occur, the child believing that this is a moment that requires a survival response.

It is natural for some adults who love the child and who know they are a safe person, to want to demonstrate this love by way of touch – a cuddle or a kiss. To children who have not been traumatised, this can be a welcome experience.

But unwanted touch, however safe it is perceived to be by the giver, can inadvertently begin to trigger trauma responses in a child who has learned that adults are not safe and touch is not safe. Without being able to vocalise their preference to whether they are cuddled or not, children rely on their safe caregivers to be their voice for them.

It is okay for a child to not want a hug, to express their boundaries and to be able to say 'No.' Until the child is able to stay in their own window of tolerance and communicate this information, it is imperative that their grown-up becomes their voice for them, modelling how to put boundaries in place and how to say 'No'.

This may be difficult to hear for the safe adult who wants to demonstrate love to the child by means of physical affection, but it is necessary in order to help the child who is learning to thrive after the onset of developmental trauma.

When Tully first came to live with me after being a street dog in Bosnia, I believed that she would appreciate having human contact immediately, knowing that I was to be her safe person. Of course, this was not the case! Tully needed to learn that she could trust me, that I would not hurt her and this took time. I would offer her my hand and sometimes she would use her paw to bring it towards her for a stroke, at other times she was dismissive of me.

I patiently had to take the cues from her and that patience paid off. Eventually, Tully stopped being dismissive of me and as her own nervous system settled, she began to enjoy the experience of being touched. However, this is limited to me and me alone! It will take more time for Tully to trust that I will not bring people around her who would not keep her safe.

I have had to stop many dog-lovers from approaching her to cuddle her; they know they won't hurt her, but she doesn't. Tully's defence is to growl and if the growl is not heard, she will bite. I quickly learned that not all dog-lovers know how to interpret the growl and it is up to me to make sure that this situation never escalates. If people can understand this about dogs who are afraid, then surely they can understand this about children who are afraid?

How to use this book

First and foremost, ensure that both you and the child are well-regulated and comfortable when you begin to read Tully's story. Make sure you choose a time when you are unlikely to be interrupted. The child may like a soother, a favourite or fidget toy, a drink or something to suck or chew to help them to stay regulated.

If the child is calm, then begins to try and distract or move away from the reading, make a note of what they have just heard in the text. It is very likely that they will have just provided you with some valuable information about something that they cannot tolerate or want to avoid for now.

The questions have been designed not only to explore the internal world of the child, but to help to develop a common language between the child and adult who are using this book together. The child cannot get the answers to the questions incorrect. Their interpretation of the thoughts and feelings Tully is having may provide some very significant information about the child's own thoughts and feelings. The child may want to expand the answers to talk about themselves and may even be able to make comparisons between Tully's feelings and their own.

Don't Touch Tully!

Tully was lying in one of her favourite places, her bed on the kitchen floor.

It had been a lovely morning so far – a good breakfast, a walk and some playing. Now Tully was stretched out, feeling the sun shining through the windows and onto her face.

Can you draw Tully?

There was only one thing that could make Tully feel happier right now, a chest rub and a cuddle from her grown-up.

Tully got up, stretched and walked into the lounge. She jumped up next to her grown-up on the comfy settee.

"Hello Tully," her grown-up said, "What do you need?"

Tully and her grown-up had an understanding. When she wanted a cuddle and a chest rub, Tully would tap her grown-up's arm with her paw and her grown-up knew what Tully wanted.

How do you let your grown-ups know what you want and need?

Are there any other ways Tully could let her grown-up know what she needs?

Tully and her grown-up sat for a while, her grown-up's arm around her, her chest being tickled. Tully put her paw on her grown-up's hand to show the grown-up that she loved them.

Tully had not always liked cuddles from her grown-up.

Tully used to live on the streets in Bosnia and some people had not been kind to Tully. This meant that Tully had found it hard to trust people.

What does trust mean?

Tully's grown-up had worked hard to show Tully that they were a grown-up who could be trusted. The grown-up did lots of things to make sure Tully knew she was safe.

What does safe mean?

The grown-up gave Tully safe food, made sure she was on a lead when they went out for a walk, gave Tully a comfortable bed and took her to the vet if she felt poorly.

What do your grown-ups do that makes you feel safe?

Tully and her grown-up knew each other very well and because Tully trusted her grown-up, when her grown-up stroked and cuddled her, it gave Tully a warm fuzzy feeling inside.

But Tully did not trust everyone, even if the grown-up said the person was safe.

When the grown-up's friend came to meet Tully for the first time, the friend walked straight up to Tully and started to stroke and tickle her.

How might Tully have felt?

Tully did not like this at all! New people gave Tully's body a big feeling and when the big feeling came, Tully's body felt prickly and spikey inside. When someone touched her when she felt prickly and spikey, it hurt Tully.

How can Tully let people know about her prickly and spikey feelings?

Tully made a clever plan. The next time the grown-up's friend came round and walked straight towards her to stroke her, Tully growled and barked and showed her teeth to the friend.

Why did Tully do this?

The plan worked and the friend stayed away from Tully. Tully was very pleased with herself. Every time Tully saw a grown-up she did not recognise, she barked and growled and bared her teeth. No one came near her!

Tully thought her plan was a good one. But sometimes she heard what people said about her. "What a horrible dog!" "Stay away from that angry dog!" "That dog does not know how to behave!"

How did this make Tully feel?

One day a strange grown-up came round to do some repairs in Tully's house. He walked towards Tully. "I love dogs!" he said. Just as he was about to get close to Tully, something happened.

"STOP!" Tully's grown-up said. "Don't touch Tully! She does not like people she does not know or trust touching her. Please leave her alone."

How might Tully feel now?

When the grown-up's friend came round the next time and walked towards Tully to cuddle her, the same thing happened. "STOP! Don't touch Tully! She does not like people she does not know or trust touching her. Please leave her alone."

Tully did not let out the growl and bark she had been preparing to do. Tully's grown-up was being her voice for her.

How does this make Tully feel?

The grown-up's friend came round some more times and on each visit, the friend did not try to touch Tully. Tully began to feel safer and safer when the friend came round. Tully watched what the friend did, so she could decide if she wanted to go near them.

What might help Tully to decide whether the grown-up is safe?

Eventually, Tully went to meet the grown-up's friend properly. She sniffed around the grown-up getting all of the information she could. Tully did not have the prickly, spikey feeling she had before. Tully held her paw out for the friend to hold.

"You can stroke her now" Tully's grown-up said.

Tully looked at her grown-up and she felt happy.

"I'm sorry I tried to cuddle you before you were ready for me to," the friend said. "I know that I am a safe person, but you did not know that and I made you feel scared. You growled and barked at me to keep yourself safe. You don't have to do that anymore. Now I know you better, I will know when I can cuddle you and when you do not want me to. It is okay if you do and it is okay if you don't, we will still be friends."

How does Tully feel now?

Tully's grown-up got Tully a special yellow lead that let other dog owners know that Tully needs space when she is on a walk. It is not okay for strangers to come and try to cuddle her.

Now when Tully is on a walk with her grown-up, she hears people say "What a lovely dog!" "What a good dog!"

Because she is.

About the author

Jess van der Hoech is a qualified therapist who has spent the last ten years studying and working with the impact of developmental trauma and, in particular, the assessment and treatment of children and adolescents with complex trauma and dissociation.

As well as supporting birth families, Jess works with looked-after and adopted children and families, using skills in attachment-focused therapy and therapeutic parenting techniques.

Jess is a supervisor, trainer and motivational speaker with a passion for writing therapeutic books that are accessible to children and families to help with the healing process and to increase awareness in the impact of trauma.

Also by Jess van der Hoech

What A Muddle (2016) ISBN 978 18381987 0 1 (Co-authored with Renée Potgieter Marks)
An interactive, practical workbook designed to help children who have difficulties with emotional regulation to begin to understand what is happening in their bodies. A variety of activities throughout the book enable the child to start to explore these ideas through the story of Sam, while gently encouraging them to begin to verbalise their own experiences. Carrying out the physical exercises in the book can promote changes in emotional regulation. The text is written in a child-friendly, gender-neutral style, and is easy to understand for parents, carers and practitioners alike. For children aged 4-12.

These Three Words (2018) ISBN 978 18381987 5 6
Also available as an e-book. A unique therapeutic novel for teenagers with the aim of linking together the feelings, emotions and behaviours connected to anxiety, with some of the therapeutic tools that can be used in order to enable better self-regulation, increased confidence and different ways of thinking. The book is equally valuable to parents of teenagers with anxiety, giving them an insight and understanding into some of the issues that may be affecting their child, and potentially opening up a line of communication and a way forward between parent and teen.

These Three Words: The Journal (2019) ISBN 978 18381987 2 5
A thought-provoking and hands-on workbook, combining a series of practical exercises and tools designed to assist teenagers who are struggling with the symptoms of anxiety. Addressing the anxious responses in both brain and body, this journal provides the reader with the opportunity to discover therapeutic coping techniques and learn how to apply them to their own personal problem areas, before committing to a twenty-eight-day practice to promote good emotional regulation and reduced anxiety. The journal can be used alongside the therapeutic novel These Three Words, or as a standalone workbook, and it is suitable for use by the teenage reader on their own, with a parent, or in a group.

Beastie, Baby and the Brand-New Mummy (2022) ISBN 978 18381987 3 2 and *Beastie, Baby and the Brand-New Daddy (2022) ISBN 978 18381987 4 9*
A therapeutic story that looks at the external signs of pathological dissociation in a child. Dolly's story helps children who have experienced early trauma to begin to understand, in a very simple way, what dissociation is and why it has happened in their internal world. Tools and techniques are included within the story that parents and caregivers can use to assist the child in the first stages of their healing process. Beautiful illustrations on every page enhance the story of Dolly, and help the reader to relate to the events that happen, to notice the methods Dolly has developed to manage her feelings, and to think about what is happening in their own internal world. For children aged 4-12

Printed in Great Britain
by Amazon